caillou®

and Gilbert

Adapted from
the animated series:
Joceline Sanschagrin
Illustrations:
CINAR Animation

chouette CINAR

One day, Caillou was coloring. He drew a big purple cat with green whiskers.
"I don't feel like drawing anymore. I want to play with a friend now," Caillou said. He left his crayons and went off to find his sister, Rosie.

There was no sound coming from Rosie's room. The shades were down and Rosie was fast asleep. Caillou tiptoed in. He knew very well that he wasn't supposed to disturb his sister when she was taking a nap.
"Rosie! Rosie!" whispered Caillou.

"Shh! Caillou, be quiet!" Startled, Caillou turned around. Daddy was calling him from the doorway.

Daddy looked annoyed. "Caillou, I've told you before not to wake Rosie when she's napping."
"I was lonely. I wanted to play with someone," Caillou explained.
"I'm sorry, but I can't play with you right now. Mommy and I are wallpapering the dining room."
"But Daddy, I'm tired of playing all by myself."
"Wait until Rosie wakes up," replied Daddy.

And he went back to help Mommy.
Caillou sighed. He didn't want to wait. He wanted someone to play with him right away.

Then Caillou saw the cat stretched out on the sofa. Gilbert didn't have any friends to play with either. "I'm going to play with Gilbert," Caillou declared happily.

He picked up the cat and put him in the back of his truck.
"Vroom! Vroom!" cried Caillou, pushing the truck.
He drove Gilbert all around the living room.
"Vroom! Vroom! Beep! Beep!"
Caillou was having a lot of fun.

The truck and the cat started going faster and faster. Whiskers back, Gilbert wondered what was going on. It was the first time in his life he had ever ridden in a truck.

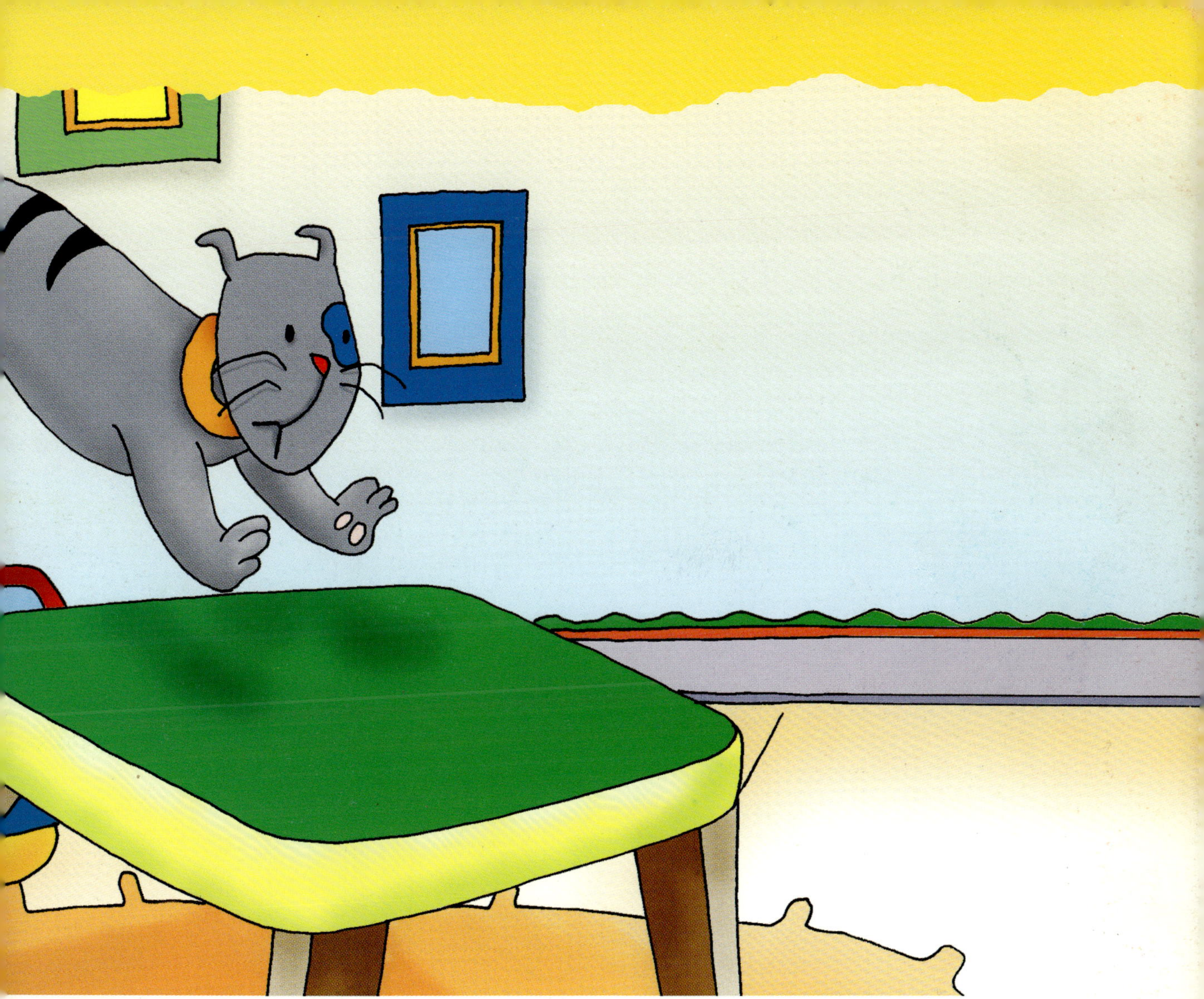

Suddenly, the truck bumped into the table. Bang!
Gilbert flew through the air and landed in a heap. Frightened, he ran and hid.

The cat didn't like the truck game. But that didn't matter, because Caillou had a better idea.
He went over to his bookshelf and picked out a book about mice. He knew Gilbert would enjoy it.

Caillou loved to tell stories. "This is a story about a little mouse called Mousy...," Caillou began in his best reading voice. He showed the picture of the mouse to Gilbert.

Gilbert scratched behind his ear. He didn't seem to be listening.

"Gilbert! Look at the cute little mouse," Caillou insisted.

Gilbert licked his paw.
He wasn't the least bit interested in Caillou's book. Caillou was losing his patience. He shoved the picture of the mouse right under Gilbert's nose.
"Gilbert! Look at this!"
The cat jumped off the sofa and ran away.

Caillou wondered what kind of stories cats did like.

"I know what we can play!" Caillou exclaimed suddenly.
He just had another idea. He went into his room and brought out some dress-up clothes. Caillou put a baby bonnet and nightgown on the cat. He burst out laughing when he saw Gilbert all dressed up like that. He put one of Daddy's old hats on his own head.

The game was all set. Caillou picked up the cat and put him gently in the stroller.

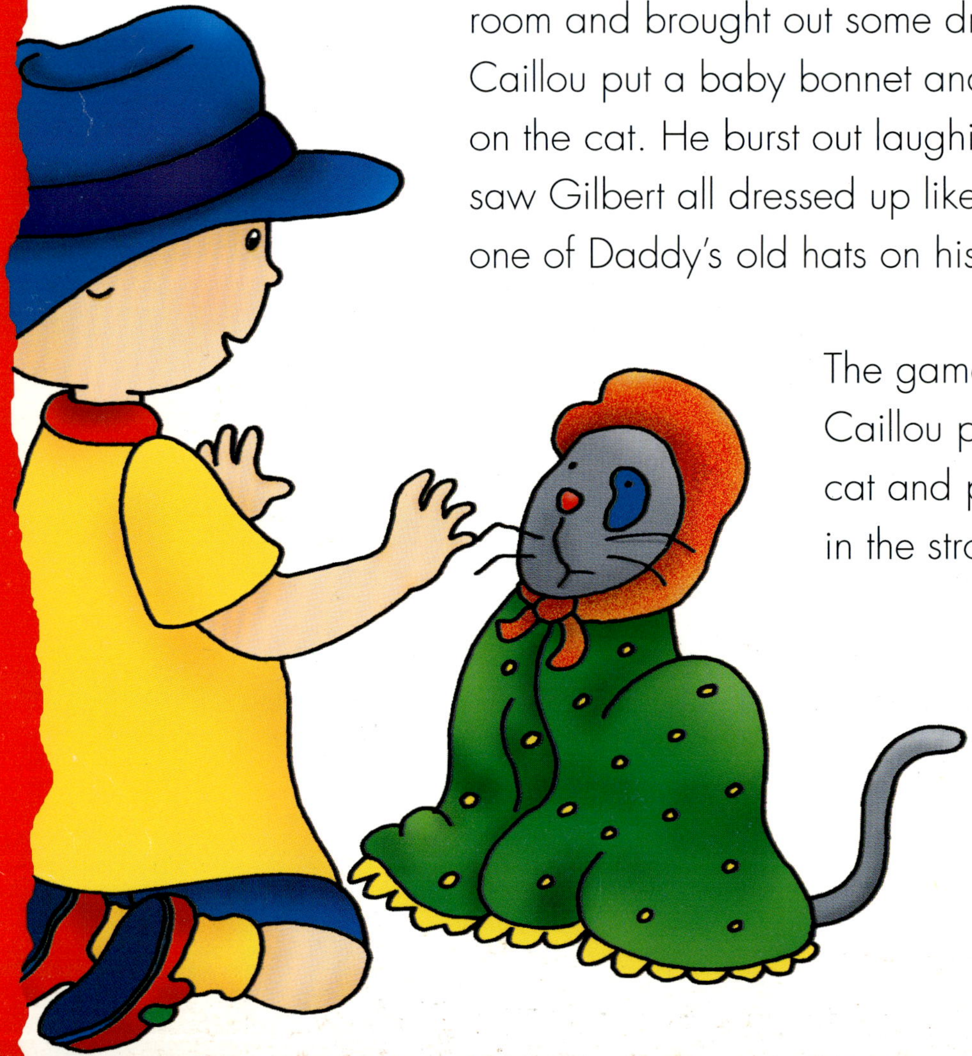

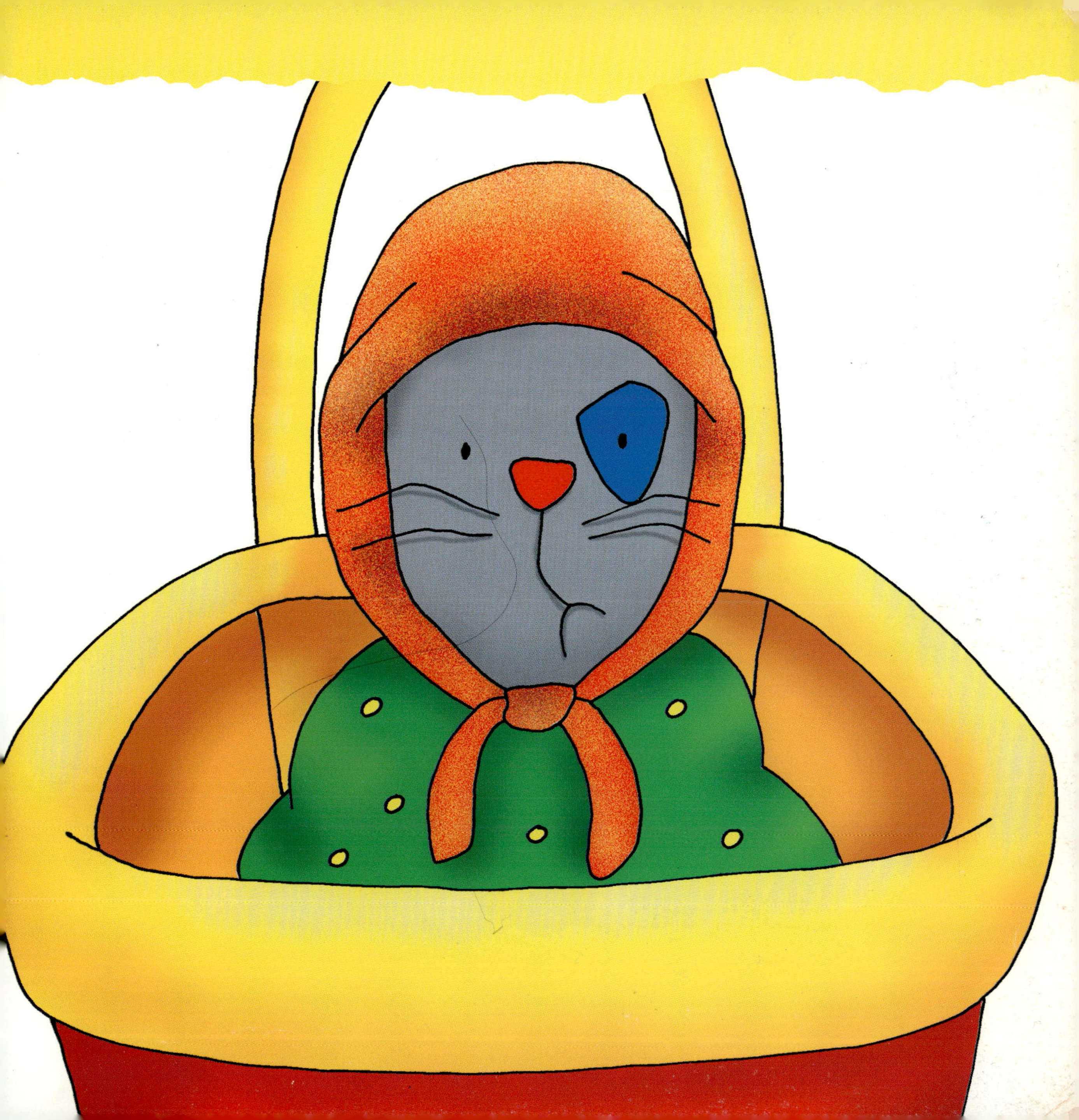

"Sit still in the stroller, Gilbert. Daddy will take you for a ride," he said. And he pushed Gilbert down the hall. But the cat didn't like being taken for a ride or being dressed up. He crouched down and then jumped out of the stroller. "Gilbert!" Caillou complained, disappointed.

The cat ran into the dining room where Mommy and Daddy were working.
"Ohh!" They were very surprised to see Gilbert in a nightgown.
"Gilbert and I were playing dress-up. I'm the daddy," Caillou explained.

"Caillou, dress-up isn't a game for animals!" said Mommy.
"Not for animals?" repeated Caillou.

"Do you like to play baby games, Caillou?" Mommy asked.
Caillou shook his head from side to side.
"That's because you're not a baby," said Mommy.
Caillou looked at her, wide-eyed, as he thought about what she had said.
"Gilbert is a cat, not a person," Mommy explained. "He likes cat games."
When Mommy went back to what she was doing, Caillou was still thinking.

"I've got it!" he said at last. "I know what Gilbert will like." Caillou undressed the cat. Then he dangled the bonnet ties in front of him. The cat's paw darted out to catch the strings. "You like cat games, don't you, Gilbert?" Caillou said happily.

"Wait for me, Gilbert. I'll be right back."
Caillou went looking for a piece of paper. He crumpled it up into a little ball and threw it to Gilbert. The cat pounced on the ball and batted it with his paw. Caillou caught it and tossed it back to the cat.
"Hurray, Gilbert! You're a champion!"

Daddy and Mommy came in to see what was going on in the living room.

Caillou was copying Gilbert. He was crawling on all fours beside him.
"We're cats. We're playing together," laughed Caillou.

Text adapted by Joceline Sanschagrin from the scenario taken from the CAILLOU animated film series produced by CINAR Corporation (© 1997 Caillou Productions Inc., a subsidiary of CINAR Corporation). All rights reserved.
Original scenario written by Christel Kleitch.
Illustrations taken from the television series CAILLOU
English translation of text: Frances Morgan
Graphic design: Monique Dupras
Computer graphics: Les Studios de la Souris Mécanique

Canadian Cataloging in Publication Data

Sanschagrin, Joceline, 1950 -
Caillou and Gilbert
(Backpack Collection)
Translation of: Caillou et Gilbert
For children ages 3 and up.
Co-published by Chouette Publishing (1987) Inc. and Cinar Corporation

ISBN 2-89450-111-0

1. Cats – Juvenile literature. 2. Children and animals – Juvenile literature.
3. Pet owners – Juvenile literature.
I. CINAR Corporation. II. Title III. Series.

SF445.7.S2613 1999 j636.8 C99-940502-0

Legal deposit: 1999

We gratefully acknowledge the financial support of BPIDP, SODEC and the Canada Council for the Arts.

Printed in Canada